GREAT

INSPIRED BY
WALTER GRETZKY

Glen Gretzky and **Lauri Holomis**

Illustrated by
Kevin Sylvester

WITH A FOREWORD BY
WAYNE GRETZKY

FOR WYATT, FOR OUR FAMILIES PRESENT AND
IN SPIRIT. . . . IN LOVING MEMORY OF GEORGIA GRACE
THANK YOU TO THE GRETZKY FAMILY

PUFFIN
an imprint of Penguin Canada Books Inc., a Penguin Random House Company

Published by the Penguin Group
Penguin Canada Books Inc., 320 Front Street West, Suite 1400, Toronto, Ontario M5V 3B6, Canada

Penguin Group (USA) LLC, 375 Hudson Street, New York, New York 10014, U.S.A.
Penguin Books Ltd, 80 Strand, London WC2R 0RL, England
Penguin Ireland, 25 St Stephen's Green, Dublin 2, Ireland (a division of Penguin Books Ltd)
Penguin Group (Australia), 707 Collins Street, Melbourne, Victoria 3008, Australia (a division of Pearson Australia Group Pty Ltd)
Penguin Books India Pvt Ltd, 11 Community Centre, Panchsheel Park, New Delhi – 110 017, India
Penguin Group (NZ), 67 Apollo Drive, Rosedale, Auckland 0632, New Zealand (a division of Pearson New Zealand Ltd)
Penguin Books (South Africa) (Pty) Ltd, 24 Sturdee Avenue, Rosebank, Johannesburg 2196, South Africa

Penguin Books Ltd, Registered Offices: 80 Strand, London WC2R 0RL, England

First published 2016

1 2 3 4 5 6 7 8 9 10   RRDA

Manufactured in China

Library and Archives Canada Cataloguing in Publication

Gretzky, Glen, author
Great / by Glen Gretzky and Lauri Holomis ; illustrated by Kevin Sylvester.
Issued in print and electronic formats.
ISBN 978-0-670-06990-3 (bound).—ISBN 978-0-14-319494-1 (epub)
1. Gretzky, Wayne, 1961– —Juvenile fiction. 2. Gretzky, Walter—Juvenile fiction.
I. Gretzky, Glen, author II. Sylvester, Kevin, illustrator III. Title.
PS8615.O46G74 2016   jC813'.6   C2015-907169-0
                                          C2015-907170-4

American Library of Congress Cataloging in Publication data available

Visit the Penguin Canada website at www.penguinrandomhouse.ca

Penguin
Random
House

FOREWORD

I'm very proud of this book and the message it gives to kids. Our Foundation's Mission Statement is about helping to equip kids for life and that begins at home. Let's ensure our kids have the encouragement, love and support they need to grow up to be strong and confident adults. Every child should know that they're Great.

Every kid deserves a shot.

Wayne Gretzky

In connection with the publication of this book, a contribution has been made to the Wayne Gretzky Foundation to help kids and families across Canada and the United States.

M om says I never get up this early.
But today is different.
Coach Wally called last night.
I MADE THE TEAM! THE BEST TEAM
IN THE WORLD!

Everyone on this team is great. They win all the time. But I'm a bit nervous. This is also *his* team. Wayne's team. The kid they are already calling the Great One.

I want to be great too.

Coach Wally is standing by the locker room, smiling.

"Welcome to the team, Taylor," he says.

"I'm going to be your best player!" I declare.

He chuckles. "As long as you have fun, work hard and do your best, that is all that matters."

Then he shows me my stall.

Everyone says hi, but I just wave.
My stomach is flopping like a goalie.
I'm right next to *him*.

Nerves.

Maybe that's why I play so badly in practice.

I try to pass the puck to Maddy. I miss her every time, by a lot.

Sam passes me the puck and it just bounces off my blade.

I'm so mad I slam my stick on the ice.

Coach Wally blows his whistle and skates over. "Taylor, just keep practicing. If you're going to do something, make sure you're focused, and do it right."

So I concentrate. I shoot pucks at my garage
again and again.
   The goalie never stops my blistering shot!
   Dad finally tells me to stop.
   But I know I'm getting better and better.

I am better at practice.
But I'm not great.
I make some bad passes.

I miss a wide-open net.
I even fall down and land on my butt.
And our first game is just a day away.

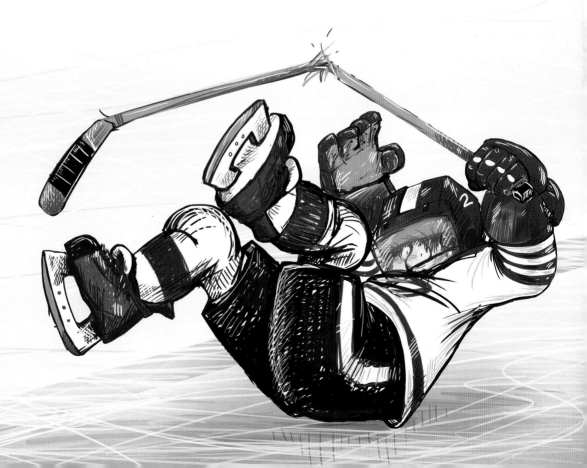

The team is great.

Wayne scores three goals in the first period.

Everyone throws hats on the ice!

I shoot on net, but it's not blistering. The goalie makes the save.

Maddy grabs the rebound and scores.

Of course we win.

She gets lots of hugs.

"Nice pass!" Wayne says to me.

"Um, thanks," I reply.

But I know it wasn't a pass.

The next game is horrible.

Wayne dekes out three players and he still has the puck!

I'm so amazed I stop skating and watch.

Wayne passes me the puck, but I miss it.

Their winger takes the puck and rushes past me.

He ties the game.

Luckily, Sam scores in overtime.

He fools the goalie and lifts it over him.

The shot knocks the water bottle off the net.

It's a great goal.

I see it from the bench.
It's great to win.
It really is.
But am I doing anything?
I don't even have a goal.

I feel useless.

I've made up my mind.

Next game, *I'm* going to be the star.

What a disaster. The game is tied. I have the puck.

I know I should pass, but I want to score.

Sam is wide open, but I take the shot myself.

It hits the defenseman's leg and bounces backward.

The other team gets a breakaway and scores.

We lose.

Lose?

I didn't think we *could* lose.

Coach Wally looks disappointed.
After the game he calls a meeting.
He says we need to keep our "heads in the game."
I know he is talking about me.

After the meeting I walk up to Coach Wally. "That game was all my fault. I think I should quit."

Coach Wally doesn't nod. He frowns. "In the middle of the season? No. You don't start something and then quit. You are part of a team."

"Yeah. The bad part of the team," I say.

He puts his hand on my shoulder and smiles. "Taylor, if you know you're not the biggest or the fastest player, you work on being the smartest. You don't have to be great *at* something to *be* great. I picked you because you worked hard. You had a great attitude. Get that back."

Great. He said my attitude was *great*. He also said *was*.

I'll make it great again.

The next game, I don't try to be the best player. I try to be the best I can be. I hope all my hard work pays off. We are tied again, and I have the puck.

But this time I don't try to score. I see that Wayne is wide open. I pass him the puck.

It isn't a great pass, but he's so good he
knocks it out of the air and into the net!

Coach Wally comes up to me.

"We wouldn't have won that game without you."

I am shocked.

"But Wayne scored the goal. It was a great goal!"

Coach smiles. "If you hadn't stolen the puck and passed it to him, he would have been out of position. You made sure he could be great, and that *we* could be great."

I feel so amazing.

It feels ... Great.